A Note to Parents

For many children, learning math is difficult and "I hate math!" is their first response — to which many parents silently add "Me, too!" Children often see adults comfortably reading and writing, but they rarely have such models for mathematics. And math fear can be catching!

The easy-to-read stories in this **Hello Reader! Math** series were written to give children a positive introduction to mathematics, and parents a pleasurable re-acquaintance with a subject that is important to everyone's life. **Hello Reader! Math** stories make mathematical ideas accessible, interesting, and fun for children. The activities and suggestions at the end of each book provide parents with a hands-on approach to help children develop mathematical interest and confidence.

Enjoy the mathematics!
• Give your child a chance to retell the story. The more familiar children are with the story, the more they will understand its mathematical concepts.
• Use the colorful illustrations to help children "hear and see" the math at work in the story.
• Treat the math activities as games to be played for fun. Follow your child's lead. Spend time on those activities that engage your child's interest and curiosity.
• Activities, especially ones using physical materials, help make abstract mathematical ideas concrete.

Learning is a messy process. Learning about math calls for children to become immersed in lively experiences that help them make sense of mathematical concepts and symbols.

Although learning about numbers is basic to math, other ideas, such as identifying shapes and patterns, measuring, collecting and interpreting data, reasoning logically, and thinking about chance, are also important. By reading these stories and having fun with the activities, you will help your child enthusiastically say "**Hello, math**," instead of "I hate math."

—Marilyn Burns
National Mathematics Educator
Author of *The I Hate Mathematics! Book*

For the good-time kids:
Tommy, James, Nolan,
Justin, and Kaitlynn
– S.M.K.

To Cindy, my sister and friend
– K.A.J.

Copyright © 1999 by Scholastic Inc.
The activities on pages 27–32 copyright © 1999 by Marilyn Burns.
All rights reserved. Published by Scholastic Inc.
SCHOLASTIC, HELLO READER! and CARTWHEEL BOOKS and associated logos
are trademarks and/or registered trademarks of Scholastic Inc.

Library of Congress Cataloging-in-Publication Data
Keenan, Sheila.
    What time is it? : a book of math riddles / by Sheila Keenan;
illustrated by K.A. Jacobs.
        p. cm. — (Hello reader! Math. Level 2)
    Summary: Illustrations and rhyming questions and answers demonstrate how to tell time.
    ISBN 0-590-12008-5
    [1. Time—Fiction. 2. Clocks and watches—Fiction. 3. Questions and answers—Fiction.
4. Stories in rhyme.] I. Jacobs, K.A., ill. II. Title. III. Series.
PZ8.3.K265Wh   1999
[E]—dc21   98-25078
                                                                     CIP
                                                                      AC

10 9 8 7 6 5 4 3 2   9/9 0/0 01 02 03 04

                          Printed in the U.S.A.   24
                          First printing, March 1999

What Time Is It?

A Book of Math Riddles

by Sheila Keenan
Illustrated by K.A. Jacobs
Math Activities by Marilyn Burns

Hello Reader! Math — Level 2

Cartwheel
·B·O·O·K·S·®

SCHOLASTIC INC.
New York   Toronto   London   Auckland   Sydney

In the middle of the day,

your stomach starts to say,

"Feed me!"

What time is it?

12:00, 12 o'clock, noon

It's after noon.

Let's have some fun.

The baseball game has just begun.

What time is it?

One is too early.

Three is too late.

If you come in between,

that would be great!

What time is it?

2:00, 2 o'clock, 2 P.M.

School is out.

Let's hop on the bus.

Wait till Mom sees

what we brought with us!

What time is it?

3:00, 3 o'clock, 3 P.M.

We went out to play at 3:30.

"Only half an hour," said Mom.

"Don't get dirty!"

Thirty minutes later,

it was time to go.

Mom took one look at us

and cried, "Oh no!"

What time is it?

4:00, 4 o'clock, 4 P.M.

The big hand is straight.

The little hand is, too.

Dinner's on the table.

(I hope it's not stew!)

What time is it?

6:00, 6 o'clock, 6 P.M.

My dog gets up early,
at half past six.
He waits half an hour
and then he does tricks.

What time is it?

7:00, 7 o'clock, 7 A.M.

Time to wake up.

Time to go to bed.

Either way, I'm a sleepyhead.

What time is it?

8 A.M. in the morning or 8 P.M. in the evening

At eight in the morning,

Dad leaves on the train.

One hour later,

he's running a crane.

What time is it?

Eight hours more and

Dad's job is all done.

Stop the crane. Catch the train.

Run, Dad, run!

What time is it?

5:00, 5 o'clock, 5 P.M.

I got up at seven
and grabbed a broom.

Three hours later,
I'm still cleaning my room!

What time is it?

10:00, 10 o'clock, 10 A.M.

"Can I try that for a minute?"

my brother asked at ten.

It took me an hour

to get my toy back again!

What time is it?

11:00, 11 o'clock, 11 A.M.

You're fast asleep.

The monsters creep.

Hands up!

What time is it?

12:00, 12 o'clock, midnight

• ABOUT THE ACTIVITIES •

"It's 7:30. Hurry with breakfast so you'll get to school on time." "Mom will be home at 5 o'clock." "You can stay up tonight until 8:30." Children often see people using clocks and watches to tell time.

While children are familiar with seeing others tell time, learning how to tell time by themselves is a complicated process. They need to learn how the hands move and how to interpret them on analog clocks and watches that have two or three hands and different kinds of numerals. They need to learn how to read the numerals on digital clocks and watches to tell the time. And they need many opportunities connecting times on all types of timekeepers to do their daily routines.

When children see the benefits of being able to tell time and want to learn to do so, it's time to help them get started. The riddles in *What Time Is It?* help by connecting telling time to children's everyday activities. After reading the riddles with your child, if your child seems interested in learning how to tell time, then use these activities to get your child started. Remember, it takes some children longer than others to learn to tell time, but all children do it eventually.

You and your child will also find the **Hello Reader! Math** books *Just a Minute* and *Monster Math School Time* useful and enjoyable for talking about time.

—Marilyn Burns

Retelling the Story

Read the first riddle again. The answer is 12 o'clock noon. When it's noon, both hands of the clock point to 12.

In the second riddle, it's one hour after noon. The time is 1 o'clock. The big hand is still on the 12, but the little hand is on the 1.

The time in the next riddle comes in between 1 o'clock and 3 o'clock, and the answer is 2 o'clock. The big hand is still on the 12 and the little hand points to the 2 this time. The big hand is always on the 12 when the time is exactly on an hour. The little hand tells what hour it is.

Next, school is out and it's 3 o'clock. How do you know?

Look carefully at the girl's wristwatch when the children are going out to play! We call this time half past three or 3:30. This means it is halfway between 3 o'clock and 4 o'clock. (On a clock with hands, the big hand would be on the 6. It would have gone halfway around the clock. The little hand would be between the 3 and the 4.)

Did you know that there are 60 minutes in an hour? Half of 60 is 30. When Mom told the children they could play for half an hour, that meant they had 30 minutes. And since it was 3:30, 30 minutes more made it exactly 4 o'clock. See where the hour and minute hands point to show 4 o'clock.

At dinnertime, the big hand on the clock points to 12 and the little hand points to 6. What time is it?

When the dog does tricks, what time is it? How do you know?

The boy is sleepy when he goes to bed at 8 o'clock at night and when he gets up at 8 o'clock in the morning. The clock looks the same each time. (See page 32 to find out why.) What time do you go to sleep? What time do you get up?

Dad leaves at 8 o'clock and it takes him one hour to get to work. What time is it then?

Dad works for eight hours. When is he finished? How do you know?

It takes the boy three hours to clean up his messy room! How does the clock show that it is 10 o'clock?

The older brother took the toy at 10 o'clock. Which of the clocks shows 10 o'clock? It took one hour for him to give back the toy. Then it was 11 o'clock. Which of the clocks shows when it was 11 o'clock?

When monsters creep, you're fast asleep! Both hands are pointing to the 12, just as they did in the first riddle, so it's 12 o'clock again. But it's nighttime, so it's midnight, not noon.

Make Your Own Clock

When a clock has hands, it needs at least two of them to tell time — one hand for the hours and the other hand for the minutes. A play clock can help you practice telling time.

• You need a paper plate, a fastener, and two strips of cardboard for the hands.

• On the paper plate, write the numbers from 1 to 12 just as they are on clocks.

• Make two clock hands from the cardboard. Make the hour hand a little shorter than the minute hand.

• Use the fastener to put the clock together.

Now read the riddles again. For each riddle, make your clock show the same time as in the picture for the riddle.

Show Me

Use your play clock to play "Show Me." Here are two different ways to play the game:

1. One person says, "Show me…" and tells a time. The other person moves the hands on the play clock to show the right time.

2. One person writes down a time, such as 10:00 or 7:00. The other person moves the hands on the play clock to show the right time.

Can you show a hard time like 3:30?

Show me 3 o'clock.

Day and Night Times

Do you remember this riddle?

> Time to wake up.
> Time to go to bed.
> Either way,
> I'm a sleepyhead.

This riddle has two possible answers — eight o'clock in the morning or eight o'clock at night. When it's eight o'clock in the morning, we write 8:00 A.M. When it's eight o'clock at night, we write 8:00 P.M.

We use "A.M." and "P.M." because every hour on the clock happens two times each day. Before 12 o'clock noon, it's "A.M." and after 12 o'clock noon, it's "P.M."

What are you usually doing at 5 o'clock A.M.? What are you usually doing at 5 o'clock P.M.? Check back in the riddles and see which times are "A.M." and which are "P.M."